THE POSSESSION

THE POSSESSION

ANNIE ERNAUX

translated by Anna Moschovakis

SEVEN STORIES PRESS
New York

Seven Stories Press
140 Watts Street
New York, NY 10013
www.sevenstories.com

College professors and high school and middle school teachers may order free exam-
ination copies of Seven Stories Press titles. To order, visit www.sevenstories.com, or
fax on school letterhead to (212) 226-1141.

Library of Congress Cataloging-in-Publication Data

Ernaux, Annie, 1940–
[Occupation, English]
The possession / Annie Ernaux ; translated by Anna Moschovakis
p. cm.
ISBN 978-1-58322-855-5 (pbk.)
I. Moschovakis, Anna. II. Title.
PQ2665.56702513 2008
843'.914--dc22

2008035106

9 8 7 6 5 4 3

[A]ND YET I KNEW THAT IF I COULD GET TO

THE END OF WHAT I WAS FEELING IT WOULD

BE THE TRUTH ABOUT MYSELF AND ABOUT THE

WORLD AND ABOUT EVERYTHING THAT ONE

PUZZLES AND PAINS ABOUT ALL THE TIME.

—Jean Rhys

I have always wanted to write as if I would be gone when the book was published. To write as if I were about to die—no more judges. Even if it's an illusion, perhaps, to believe that truth comes only by way of death.

The first thing I did after waking up was grab his cock—stiff with sleep—and hold still, as if hanging onto a branch. I'd think, "as long as I'm holding this, I am not lost in the world." Now, when I think about the significance of that sentence, it seems to me that what I meant was there is nothing to wish for but this, to have my hand wrapped around this man's cock.

Now he's in the bed of another woman. Maybe she makes the same gesture, stretching out her hand and grabbing his cock. For months, I have had a vision of this hand and have felt that it was mine.

———

And yet I was the one who had left W., several months earlier, after six years together—as much out of boredom as from an inability to give up my freedom, reclaimed after eighteen years of marriage, for the shared life he so strongly desired from the start. We continued to talk on the phone; we saw each other from time to time. He called me one evening, told me he was moving out of his studio, he was going to be living with a woman. From then on there would be rules about calling each other (only on his cell phone) and about seeing each other (no nights or weekends). I was gripped by a sense of disaster, out of which something else emerged. At that moment, the existence of this other woman took hold of me. All of my thoughts passed through her.

This woman filled my head, my chest, and my gut; she was always with me, she took control of my emotions. At the same time, her omnipresence gave my life a new intensity. It produced stirrings that I had never felt before, released a kind of energy, powers of imagination I didn't know I had; it held me in a state of constant, feverish activity.

I was, in both senses of the word, possessed.

This state kept my daily troubles and cares at bay. In a way, it placed me outside the grip of life's usual mediocrity. But any reflection that politics or current events would normally arouse in me was lost, too. I've tried and tried: apart from the Concorde crashing after take-off into a certain Hotelissimo de Gonesse, nothing in the world from the summer of 2000 left behind a memory.

There was suffering, on the one hand; and on the other, a mind incapable of applying itself to anything but the testimony and analysis of that suffering.

I absolutely had to know her name, her age, her profession, her address. I discovered that these details by which society defines a person's identity, which we so easily dismiss as irrelevant to truly knowing someone, are in fact essential. They were the only way for me to extract a physical and social type from the undifferentiated mass of womankind; to conjure up a body, a lifestyle; to construct the image of an individual person. And as soon as he told me—grudgingly—that she was forty-seven years old; that she was a professor, divorced with a sixteen-year-old daughter; and that she lived on Avenue Rapp in the Seventh arrondissement, a silhouette emerged of a trim woman in a crisp blouse, her hair impeccably styled, preparing for class at a desk in a softly lit bourgeois apartment.

The number 47 took on a strange materiality. I saw the two digits, giant, all around me. I began to see women solely for their position in the march of time and of the aging process, the effects of which I would compare to my own. Any woman who appeared to fall between forty and fifty years old and who dressed with the req-uisite "elegant simplicity" of the finer neighborhoods became a stand-in for the other woman.

I discovered that I hated all female professors—though I myself had been one, and many of my friends still were. I found them aggressive, unyielding: a return to the perception I'd had in high school when I was so intimidated by my women teachers I thought I would never be able to do what they did, to be like them. I saw the body of my enemy replicated in every member of the teaching body, which had never worn its name so well.

In the Métro, any woman in her forties carrying a shopping bag was "her," and just to look at her was to suffer. I resented the indifference of these women to my gaze, the way one would rise in a rather brisk, decisive motion from her seat and exit the train at a station (the name of which I would duly note)—it was like a denial of my being, a way for this woman, whom I'd taken throughout the train ride to be W.'s new lover, to give me the finger.

One day, I found myself remembering J.—with the brilliant eyes and mass of curly hair—bragging about having orgasms in her sleep that would wake her up. And instantly, the other woman took her place; I saw this other woman, heard her, exuding sensuality and repeated orgasms. It was as if an entire class of women with extraordinary erotic capabilities—the arrogant, radiant women whose photos adorn the covers of the magazines' "Summer Sex" issues—all stood up triumphantly, and I was excluded.

This transubstantiation of the bodies of women I encountered into the body of the other woman was in continual operation: I saw her everywhere.

If—while glancing through the classifieds in *Le Monde*, or the real estate section—I came across a mention of Avenue Rapp, this reminder of the street on which the other woman lived would so brutally overshadow the rest of my reading that I would understand nothing that came after it. There was now a territory—with borders stretching vaguely from Invalides to the Eiffel Tower, encompassing the Pont de l'Alma and the posh, White part of the Seventh arrondisement—which nothing in the world could convince me to enter. A zone always present inside me, completely contaminated by the other woman, which the bright spotlight atop the Eiffel Tower—visible from the windows of my house in the heights of the western suburbs—obstinately revealed to me, bathing it in light at regular intervals every evening until midnight.

When for some reason I had to go into the Latin Quarter—the part of Paris, other than the Avenue Rapp, where I ran the highest risk of running into him in the company of the other woman—I had the uncanny feeling that I was in a hostile environment, being watched from all sides. It was as if, in this neighborhood which I had filled with the other woman's existence, there was no room left for my own. I felt like a fraud—to walk down the Boulevard Saint Michel or the Rue Saint Jacques, even when I had good reason to, was to expose my desire to run into them. With its vast, accusatory gaze bearing down on me, all of Paris punished me for this desire.

The strangest thing about jealousy is that it can populate an entire city—the whole world—with a person you may never have met.

During the rare moments of respite when I felt as I had before, when I was able to think of other things, the image of this woman would suddenly tear through me. I had the feeling that it wasn't my brain producing this image, that it burst in from somewhere else. It was as if this woman could enter and exit my head at will.

In the private film that was constantly playing inside me—featuring happy moments to come, a night out, a vacation, a birthday dinner—all of this autofiction anticipating the pleasures of a normal life was supplanted by the images that were rushing in from the outside to stab me in the chest. I was no longer free in my daydreams. I was no longer the subject even of my own fantasies. I was being inhabited by a woman I had never seen. Or, to borrow the word of a Senegalese man who once told me he was being possessed by an enemy, I was "maraboutée."

I only felt free from this grip when I was trying on the dress or the pair of pants I had just bought in anticipation of my next meeting with W. His imagined gaze returned me to myself.

I began to suffer from our separation.

When I wasn't preoccupied with the other woman, I fell prey to the attacks of an outside world bent on reminding me of our common past, which now felt to me like an irremediable loss.

Suddenly, without relief and at a dizzying speed, pictures from our relationship appeared in my memory, like the movie montages in which the images stack and overlap but never disappear. Streets, cafes, hotel rooms, overnight trains, and beaches spun around, merged. An avalanche of scenes and landscapes, the reality of which was chilling: I was there. I felt as if my brain was freeing itself, in relentless spurts, of all the images it had collected over the course of my relationship with W., and I couldn't do anything to stop the flow. As if the world from those years—because I hadn't savored its unique flavor—was taking its revenge by returning, determined to devour me. At times I thought I would go crazy from the pain. But the pain was actually a sign that I was not crazy. To make this monstrous carousel stop, I knew I could pour myself a stiff drink or swallow a tablet of Imovane.

For the first time, I could clearly perceive the material nature of feelings and emotions—I physically felt their consistency, their form but also their independence, their perfect freedom with respect to my consciousness. These interior states had their equivalent in nature: the surge of a wave, the crumbling of a cliff, sinkholes, algae blooms. I understood the necessity of comparisons and metaphors using water and fire. Even the most overused of them had first been *lived,* one day, by someone.

Continually, songs or news reports on the radio, advertisements, would plunge me back into the time of my relationship with W. Hearing "Happy Wedding," "*Juste quelqu'un de bien,*" or an interview with Ousmane Sow, whose colossal statues on the Pont des Arts we had seen together, put a catch in my throat. Any evocation of a separation or a departure—one Sunday it was a host leaving FIP, the radio station where she had worked for thirty years—was enough to wreck me completely. Like people made fragile by disease or depression, I was an echo chamber for all pain everywhere.

One night, on the RER platform, I thought of Anna Karenina at the moment when she was about to throw herself under the train, with her little red bag.

Above all I remembered the first moments of our affair, the "magnificence" of his cock, as I had noted in my diary. It wasn't the other woman, in the end, whom I saw in my place—it was me, the way that I never would be again, in love and sure of his love, on the threshold of everything that hadn't yet taken place between us.

I wanted him *back*.

———

I absolutely had to see a certain film on TV, under the pretext that I had missed it in the theater. But then I had to admit that wasn't the reason at all. I had missed countless films and remained indifferent to their subsequent showings on television several years later. If I wanted to watch *L'ecole de la chair*, it was because of a similarity between what I knew of the film's story—a penniless young man with a well-heeled older woman—and the experience I'd had with W., which the other woman was now having with him.

Whatever the script, if the heroine was in pain, it was my pain that was being portrayed, worn on the actress's body in a kind of doubling that oppressed me. So much so that I was almost relieved when the film was over. One evening, I thought I had sunk to the depths of despair with a Japanese film in black and white, set in the postwar years, in which it rained without stopping. I told myself that six months earlier I would have seen the same film with pleasure, deriving a deep satisfaction from the spectacle of a sorrow I was not experiencing. De facto, catharsis only benefits those who are untouched by passion.

Hearing by chance "I Will Survive," a song to which—
long before it was belted out in the locker rooms of the
World Cup—I would sometimes let loose dancing in
W's apartment, I was petrified. Back when I was
twirling around him, all that mattered were the rhythm
of the music and the fierce voice of Gloria Gaynor,
which felt to me like the victory of love over time. In
the supermarket where I heard it between two com-
mercials, the singer's refrain took on a new, desperate
meaning; me too, I must, *I will survive.*

———

He had not wanted to tell me her name.

This absent name was a hole, a void around which I
turned in circles.

During the encounters we continued to have, in cafes
or at my house, he would answer my reiterated ques-
tions—presented sometimes in the form of a game
("Tell me the first letter of her first name")—with a

refusal to let me "force it out of him" accompanied by a "What good would it do you to know?" And while ready to argue vigorously that the desire to know is the essence of life and of intelligence, I would concede "nothing," while thinking "everything." When I was in grade school, I absolutely had to know the name of this or that girl from another class whom I liked to watch during recess. When I was an adolescent, it was the name of a boy I passed frequently in the street and whose initials I engraved in the wooden desk. It seemed to me that to *put a name* to this woman would allow me to construct, out of what is always awakened by a word and its sounds, a personality type: to hold an image of her—even if a completely false one—inside me. To know the name of the other woman was, in my own deficiency of being, to own a little part of her.

I saw in his obstinate refusal to give me her name or to describe her even the slightest bit a fear that I would become angry at her in a violent or twisted way, that I would cause a scandal (and thus a presumption that I was capable of the worst—a revolting idea that increased my distress). At certain moments, I also suspected a kind of mawkish cunning, a will to maintain me in a state of frustration that would keep alive the newfound desire I had for him. At others, I saw a desire to protect her, to remove her completely from my thoughts, as if they would be detrimental to her. Whereas, realistically, he was acting out of a habit—developed in childhood to hide the alcoholism of his father from his friends—to lie about everything, even the details least likely to provoke the judgment of others, in a sort of permanent "what you don't know can't hurt me" from which he drew his strength as a shy but proud person.

The search for the name of the other woman became an obsession, a need to be satisfied by any means necessary.

I managed to extort a few pieces of information

from him. The day he told me she was a lecturer in history at Paris-III, I rushed to the Internet to visit the university's website. When I saw among the sections one which listed the instructors classified by specialty, with phone numbers next to their names, I experienced a sensation of unbelievable happiness—immoderate—which no discovery of an intellectual nature could have provided me at that moment. I scrolled down the screen, slowly becoming disenchanted: Even though in history the women were far less numerous than the men, I had nothing specific to help me locate her in the list.

Every new clue I extracted from him propelled me immediately into a tortuous and relentless search of the Internet, the use of which suddenly became important to my life. So, when he let on that she had written her doctoral dissertation on the Chaldeans, I launched the search engine—aptly named, I thought—on the word "dissertation." After a number of clicks on different links—specialization, place of doctoral work—the name appeared of one of the instructors I had already found in the list of professors of Ancient History at Paris-III. I sat there frozen before the letters inscribed on the screen. The existence of this woman had become a reality, indestructible and atrocious. It was like a statue emerging from the mud. Afterward, a kind of peacefulness came over me, accompanied by an empty feeling similar to the one that comes after taking an exam.

A little later I was assailed by doubt, and I consulted the Minitel directory. After multiple searches, I discovered that the teacher in question didn't live in Paris but in Versailles. It was therefore not "her."

Every time I was struck by a new hypothesis about the identity of the other woman, the violence of the thought's eruption—the hollow pit in my chest, the heat in my hands—seemed to be an indication of certainty as irrefutable as inspiration is, perhaps, for a poet or a scholar.

One evening, I felt this certainty with respect to another name from the list of professors and searched immediately on the Internet to see if the one with that name had published any books having anything to do with the Chaldeans. In the section about her there was this: "*Translating the relics of Saint Clement*, article in progress." I was flooded with joy; I imagined myself saying to W. with devastating irony, "the translation of the relics of Saint Clement, what a scintillating subject!" or "Here's the text the entire world has been waiting for! That will change the world!" etc. Testing out all the variants of a sentence meant to ridicule the other woman's work to death. Until other indications challenged the notion that she might be the author of this article—beginning with the glaring absence of any relationship between the Chaldeans and Saint Clement, Pope and martyr.

I imagined calling all the numbers of the teachers, which I had carefully noted, and asking—after taking the precaution of first dialing 36 51, which blocks caller ID—"May I speak to W.?" And if I got the right number and the reply was "yes," I would blurt out in a crass voice, making use of some detail he had let slip out of concern for a physical ailment of hers, "So, pretty lady, how about that piece-of-shit bladder of yours?" before hanging up.

In these moments, I felt a primordial savagery rise up inside me. I caught glimpses of all the acts I would have been capable of if society hadn't constrained my impulses; for example, instead of simply looking up the name of this woman on the Internet, shooting her with a revolver while screaming "Bitch! Bitch! Bitch!" Something I had done at times, at the top of my voice, without the revolver. My suffering, at base, was about not being able to kill her. And I envied the primitive morals of brutish societies whereby one would kidnap the person or even assassinate her, resolving the situation in minutes and avoiding the prolongation—which appeared to me end-less—of suffering. Suddenly I understood the leniency of the courts toward so-called crimes of passion, their loathing to apply a law that tells us to punish murderers, a law derived from reason and necessity but which runs counter to another more visceral one: the right to eliminate the man or woman who has taken over your body and your mind. Their desire, at base, not to condemn the final act of a person who is prey to an intolerable suffering, the act of Othello and of Roxanne.

I was trying to regain my freedom, to get rid of this weight inside me, and everything I did was in the service of this goal.

I remembered the girl W. had left when he met me and how she had said to him, in a rage, "I will stick you with needles!" The idea of making dolls out of bread dough and pricking them with pins no longer seemed so ridiculous to me. At the same time, the image of my hands pummeling the dough, pricking carefully where the head or the heart would be, was the image of another person, of a poor naïf: I could not "sink so low." But the temptation was somehow attractive and scary, like leaning over a well and watching your reflection tremble at the bottom.

The act of writing, here, is perhaps not so different from that of sticking needles.

In a general sense, I became accepting of behaviors that had formerly been stigmatized for me or that had provoked my ridicule. "How could anyone do that?!"

became "I could see myself doing that." I compared my attitude and my obsession to certain current events, like the young woman who had harassed a former lover and his new companion for years on the telephone, clogging their answering machine, etc. Just as I saw W.'s woman in dozens of others, I projected myself into all those who—crazier or more audacious than me—had in any way "blown a fuse."

(It's possible that, unbeknownst to me, my story serves the same exemplary role.)

During the day, I was able to suppress my desires. When night fell, so would my defenses, and my need to know would come back, more invasive than ever, as if it had only been put to sleep by the day's events, or temporarily reduced by reason. I would give in to it with all the more abandon, having restrained myself all day. It was a reward that I would offer myself for having "behaved" for so long, like obese people who have scrupulously followed their diet since morning and in the evening allow themselves a chocolate bar.

The thing I most wanted to do—to call "everyone" in the building where she lived with W. (I had found their names and numbers on the Minitel)—was also the most terrifying. It would allow me to kill two birds with one stone: access the existence in reality of this woman, while listening to a voice that might be hers.

One evening, I methodically dialed each number, preceded by 36 51. There were answering machines, unanswered rings; from time to time an unknown male voice would answer and say hello, and I'd hang up. When it was a woman I would ask for W., in a tone both neutral and determined, and then before there was time for a negative or alarmed reply, I would exclaim that I had dialed the wrong number. This leap from plan to action was exalting in its illicitness. I made scrupulous notes next to each number I called—male or female, answering machine, hesitation. One woman hung up immediately after my question, without a word. I was certain it was her. But later, this didn't seem to be sufficient evidence. "She" could have an unlisted number.

Among the names that I called, one woman had left the number of her cell phone on her answering machine: Dominique L. Determined not to pass up any chance, I dialed it the next morning. A happy female voice, the kind that betrays eagerness and the joy of receiving a call, chimed "Hello?" I remained silent. The voice on the phone, suddenly on guard, repeated "hello" compulsively. Finally I hung up without saying anything, embarrassed and amazed to have discovered such a simple demonic power, that of sending someone into a panic from afar, with complete impunity.

Whether my compulsions or my conduct were digni-
fied was not a question I asked myself on that occasion,
no more than I ask it now as I write this. I have come to
believe that only in its absence can one come close to
the truth.

In the state I was in, of uncertainty and the need to
know, the most tangential clues could become brutally
relevant. My talent for connecting the most disparate
facts into a relation of cause and effect was prodigious.
For instance, the evening after he postponed a meeting
we had planned for the following day, when I heard at
the end of the weather report the announcement that
tomorrow we will celebrate Dominique, I was sure that
was the name of the other woman: he couldn't come to
my place because it was her name day, and they would
be going together to a restaurant, a candlelight dinner,
etc. This reasoning came to me like a flash of lighting.
I could not doubt it. My hands suddenly frozen, my

blood "that ran cold" when I heard *Dominique* were my proof of its validity.

One could find in this hunt and this frantic assembling of signs an exercise in the abandonment of intelligence. But I see its having a poetic function—the same one that is at work in literature, religion, and paranoia.

And anyway, I am writing jealousy as I lived it, tracking and accumulating the desires, sensations, and actions that were mine during this period. It's the only way for me to make something real of my obsession. And I am always afraid to let something essential escape. Writing, that is, as a jealousy of the real.

———

One morning, F.—a friend of my son's—called me. She had moved and gave me her new address, in the 12th arrondisement. Her landlady had asked her for tea, loaned her some books: *she's a professor of History at*

Paris-III. These words, arising in the middle of a casual conversation, had the effect on me of a blinding piece of luck. Just like that, after weeks of fruitless research, the childish voice of F. was offering me the chance to know the name of the other woman, a professor of the same subject on the same campus as her landlady. But I judged it impossible to involve F. in my quest, to expose a curiosity whose unusual, obviously illicit nature would not escape her. Once we had hung up, although determined not to succumb to it, I wasn't able to get rid of the temptation to call F. back and ask her to question her landlady about the other woman. Against my will, the first words of an introduction to the matter for F. were forming in my head. Within a few hours, the will of a desire impatient to be satisfied overpowered my fear of being exposed; that evening, in that perverse state of mind in which you convince yourself that what you are about to do is not only harmless, but necessary, I dialed F.'s number with determination, ardently hoping that she would be home, that I would not have to put off my quest and that I would have the chance to deliver the sentence I'd been rehearsing all afternoon: "F., I have something to ask you! Something out of a novel! Would you happen to know the name of. . . ," etc.

As with every other time when I thought I had reached my goal, after assigning the research task to F. I felt weary, drained, almost indifferent to the wait, even to the eventual result. The latter inspired new suspicions: the landlady claimed to have no idea which professor I could be referring to. I thought that she was lying, that she knew this woman, that she too wanted to protect her.

I wrote in my journal "I have decided not to see him again." At the moment when I wrote these words I was no longer suffering, and I confused the relief of my suffering—through writing—with the end of my feelings of loss and jealousy. No sooner had I closed my notebook than I was gripped by the desire to know the name of this woman, to find out information about her—all the things that would go on to create more suffering.

When he was at my house and he went into the bathroom, I was irresistibly drawn toward his briefcase sitting in the entryway. I was sure that it concealed everything I wanted to know: the name, the telephone number, maybe a photo. I would approach it silently and stand fascinated in front of this black object, not breathing, filled with desire and with the incapacity to touch it. I saw myself fleeing with it to the back of the garden, opening it and extracting its contents one by one, throwing them all over until, like a purse snatcher, I found my treasure.

It would, obviously, have been easy for me to learn the identity of this woman by going in secret to her address on Avenue Rapp. To get past the first obstacle, a door that would open only with a code I didn't have, I had imagined making an appointment with the gynecologist who practiced in the building. But I dreaded being seen by him, or by the two of them together, thus revealing all my dereliction, that of a woman no longer loved, exposing my desire to be loved again. I could have paid a detective. But that also would mean showing my desire to someone whose profession I did not hold in high esteem. It occurs to me that I wanted to be indebted to no one but myself—or chance—for the discovery of this woman's name.

The exhibition that I am making here—by writing—of my obsession and my suffering is completely unlike what I feared in showing up at Avenue Rapp. To write, first of all, is not to be seen. As inconceivable, as atrocious, as it seemed to me to offer up my face, my body, my voice—everything that made up the singularity of my being—to the gaze of anybody while in the state of consumption and abandon I was in, today I feel no embarrassment whatever—still less, any resistance—about exposing and exploring my obsession. To tell the truth, I am *going through* absolutely nothing. I am simply forcing myself to describe the appearance and behavior of this jealousy which took root in me, to transform the individual and intimate into a sensible, intelligible substance that unknown persons, irrelevant at the moment I am writing, might make their own. It is no longer *my* desire, *my* jealousy, in these pages—it is *of* desire, *of* jealousy; I am working in invisible things.

———

When I called him on his cell phone—he had not, naturally, given me his number at the other woman's place—he would sometimes exclaim "I was just thinking about you, just this minute!" Far from making me happy, making me believe in some spiritual connection, this remark would throw me. I heard in it only one thing: The rest of the time, I was not on his mind. Which was precisely what I would not be able to say: from morning till night, he—and she—did not leave mine.

In conversation, he would sometimes toss out an incidental "Didn't I tell you?" which he would follow up, without waiting for a reply, with the retelling of an event that had occurred in his life in the preceding days, the announcement of some news concerning his work. This false question instantly deflated me. It meant that he had *already* told whatever it was to the other woman. She was the one who, because of her proximity, was the first to hear everything that happened to him, from the trivial to the essential. I was *always* the second—at best—to be informed. This opportunity to share, in the moment, what is happening, what one is thinking, which plays such a big role in the comfort of couples and in their longevity—I was deprived of it. "Didn't I tell you?" placed me in the sphere of friends and of people one sees from time to time. I was no longer the first and indispensable trustee of his daily life. "Didn't I tell you?" reminded me of my function as an occasional ear. "Didn't I tell you?" was the same as: I didn't need to tell you.

During this time, I relentlessly carried on that interior narrative, woven together from things seen and heard throughout the day, that one constructs for the beloved in his absence—the description of my daily life which, I quickly realized, no longer interested him.

That with all the possibilities available to a man in his thirties he would choose a woman of forty-seven was intolerable to me. I saw in this choice the clear proof that he had loved me not as the singular being I'd believed I was in his eyes, but only as a mature woman with her typical assets: financial independence, a stable position, and experience—or perhaps taste, a maternal quality, and sexual tenderness. I realized that I was an interchangeable part of a series. I could just as well have reversed the reasoning and admitted that the advantages of his youth played some role in my attachment to him. But I had no urge to place myself under objective scrutiny. In my elation and the force of my bad-faith argument, I found a defense against hopelessness.

The superiority that I could have felt with respect to this woman—during certain social occasions, due to recognition for my work—I saw from the outside. This vision of others, their gaze, which it is so fortifying to perform for, to notice; which flatters one's vanity so well; was powerless against her existence. In the self-erasure that is the state of jealousy, which transforms every difference into a lack, it was not only my body, my face, that were devalued but also my occupation—my entire being. I went so far as to be mortified that at the other woman's house he was able to watch the TV channel Paris Première, which I could not receive. And I saw a sign of intellectual distinction, a mark of superior indifference to practical things, in the fact that she did not know how to drive and had never gotten her license, while I had been overjoyed to get mine at twenty to go sunbathe in Spain with the rest of the world.

My one source of pleasure was to imagine the other woman finding out he still saw me—that he'd just, *for example*, given me a bra and g-string for my birthday. I experienced a physical release, I bathed in the bliss of truth being revealed. Finally, suffering had switched bodies. I temporarily relieved my own pain by imagining hers.

One Saturday night on the Rue Saint-André-des-Arts, I remembered past weekends we had spent in that neighborhood, without particular joy, having resigned ourselves to a ritual without surprises. It must have been, then, that the image of the Other—the desire that this Other had for him—was equipped with a force great enough to sweep away the boredom and everything that had compelled me to break things off. At that moment, I realized that ass—in this case the ass of the other woman—was the most important thing in the world.

Today, it makes me write.

Without a doubt the greatest suffering, like the greatest happiness, comes from the Other. I understand that some people fear this and try hard to avoid it by loving with moderation, by favoring a match made of common interests, music, political engagement, a house with a garden, etc.; or with multiple sexual partners who are seen as objects of pleasure separate from the rest of life.

And yet, if my suffering seemed absurd to me—outrageous, even, when compared to others both physical and social—if it seemed a luxury, I still preferred it to certain calm and productive periods in my life.

It even seemed to me that having gone through the phases of school and of relentless work, marriage and reproduction; having more or less paid my debt to society; I was finally devoting myself to what was essential and had been lost from view since adolescence.

———

Nothing he said was insignificant. In "I worked at the Sorbonne" I heard "They worked together at the Sorbonne." All of his sentences were subject to an incessant de-coding, to interpretations whose unverifiability made them agonizing. The ones to which I paid no attention at first would return at night to ravage me with meanings that were suddenly hopelessly clear. The functions of exchange and communication that are generally ascribed to language had receded into the background, replaced by a singular function capable of signifying only one of two things: his love for me or for the other woman.

I made a list of grievances toward him. Every reproach I wrote down brought with it an intense and fleeting sense of satisfaction. When he called me a few days later, I gave up the idea of enumerating this overwhelming tally of wrongs, suspecting that one doesn't acknowledge such things without the hope that the acknowledgment will have some benefit. He didn't want anything more from me, except perhaps for me to leave him alone.

With the remarkable ability of desire to use as evidence anything that serves it, I shamelessly appropriated the clichés and received ideas that idled in the magazines. And so I persuaded myself that this woman's daughter would not stand for the presence of a lover much younger than her mother, or that she would fall in love with him herself, life together would become untenable, etc.

While walking or doing some repetitive household chore, I constructed arguments to demonstrate how he had fallen into a trap, why he should return to me. Internal dissertations in which the chapters flowed without effort and without end, in a rhetorical fever that no other subject would have aroused. The erotic scenes I replayed interminably at the beginning of our relationship and which I avoided thinking about now because they could not be realized, all the dreams of pleasure and happiness, had given way to a sterile and arid discourse of persuasion. Its artificial character became apparent to me when, after I'd managed to reach him on his cell phone, he reduced my logical construction to nothing with a sober and clear-sighted, "I don't like it when people pressure me."

The only thing that was true, and I never said it to him, was "I want to fuck you and make you forget the other woman." All the rest was, literally, fiction.

In my argumentative strategies, one sentence stood out which seemed dazzling in its truth: "You accept the subjection of this woman like you never would have accepted mine." This truth seemed all the more irrefutable since it was fueled by the desire to hurt him, to force him to rebel against a dependence that I had made him see. I was satisfied with the choice of words, with the concise formulation, and I would have liked to drop my "bomb" of a sentence right then, to transport my well-crafted, perfect retort from the theater of the imagination to the theater of real life.

To do something at all costs and to do it right away, without enduring the slightest delay. I experienced this law of urgency, which typifies states of madness and of suffering, constantly. To have to wait for the next call before clobbering him with the truth I had just discovered and formulated for myself was intolerable. As if this truth might gradually cease to be one as the days went by.

At the same time, there was the hope of relieving my pain with a phone call, a letter, the return of pictures of us together—to put it, definitively, "behind me." But possibly still, at base, the desire not to succeed, to hold onto this suffering which, after all, gave meaning to the world. Because the true goal of these actions was to force him to react and thereby maintain a painful bond.

Often, the urgency to act in one way or another was accompanied by feverish deliberations. To write or to telephone. Today, tomorrow, in a week. To say this rather than that. In the end, perhaps suspecting the inefficacy of it all, I would resort to drawing lots with cards or little folded pieces of paper which I picked while closing my eyes. The satisfaction—or, on the other hand, the regret—that I felt upon reading the response served to inform me of my real desire.

If I managed not to succumb to the urgency, and to defer for a day or two the phone call I was burning to make, my forced voice, the words that came out too slowly or aggressively, ruined the intended effect of the delay—which, I noticed, W. saw for what it was: a transparent ploy.

And when faced with his refusal to engage, with the inertia of a man caught between two women, a blast of rage blew away my powers of argument and my masterful use of language: On the verge of letting my pain flood out in insults—"stay there, you big jerk, with your fat cow"—I collapsed into tears.

One Sunday afternoon, I went to the theater with L., who was visiting France and whom I hadn't seen in seven years. Afterward, we made love on the couch in his parents' living room, with a series of gestures that came back on their own. He told me I was beautiful and that I gave excellent head. In my car, driving back to my house, I thought that it wasn't enough to free me. The "purging of the passions" that I often hope for from the sexual act—and which a Carribean song seemed to explain so well: "Ah! Just stick your prick inside me / And get it over with / Ah! (etc.) / Let's not talk about it anymore"—did not occur.

[I had expected everything from sexual pleasure, especially from him. Love and connection; access to the infinite; the desire to write. The best I seemed to have acquired so far was lucidity: a new vision—suddenly simple and de-sentimentalized—of the world.]

———

In the fall, during a multi-disciplinary colloquium at

which I was speaking, I noticed a woman in the second row of the audience—short brown hair, seemingly petite, a severe and elegant size 40, wearing a dark suit—whose eyes kept wandering in my direction. A leather bag that tied in the back was set down next to her seat. I was sure right away that it was her. As the other panelists spoke, our eyes kept meeting in the split-second before we could both look away. When it was time for the discussion, she requested the floor. With ease, in a voice full of mastery, she asked a question relevant to my talk but addressed it to another speaker. This way of conspicuously ignoring me constituted devastating proof: It was her. Having read my name on a flyer for the colloquium that would have been posted in the universities, she wanted to see what I looked like. In a low voice I asked the panelists on my right and my left who this woman was. Neither one knew her. She did not return in the afternoon. From that moment on, I saw the other woman in the anonymous dark of the colloquium. It gave me some peace, even some pleasure. Then I began to think that the clues were insufficient. My conviction was based less on these clues—though unmistakable, there were witnesses—than on my having found in this silent room of the university colloquium a body, a voice, and a haircut conforming to the image that I carried around in me; on having found the ideal type that I had fabricated and, for months, detested. There was as good a chance that the other woman was shy, with blond curly hair, a size 44 dressed in red, but I just could not believe it—that picture had never existed in my head.

One Sunday, I was walking through the empty streets of the center of P. The portail du Carmel was open. I went through for the first time. A man was stretched out along the ground, face to the earth, his arms crossed, chanting loudly in front of a statue. Next to the pain that was wrenching this man, mine did not seem real.

The thought occurred to me sometimes, in a flash, that if he were suddenly to say "I'm leaving her and coming back to you," after a minute of absolute happiness—of almost unbearable elation—I would feel an exhaustion, a mental depletion comparable to that of the body after orgasm, and I would wonder why I had wanted this thing.

———

The image of his cock on the other woman's belly came up less frequently than that of a daily life that he evoked carefully in the singular and I heard always in the plural. It was not the erotic gestures that would bind him most to her (these happened all the time and without consequence on the beach, in the corner of an office, in rooms rented by the hour), but the baguette that he would bring home for her at lunchtime, their underwear mingled together in the laundry basket, the television show that they watched in the evenings while eating spaghetti bolognaise. Out of my sight, a process of domestication, slow and sure, had begun to grip him tightly; with the shared breakfasts and tooth-brushes in the same glass, a mutual impregnation that he seemed to wear, physically, in an impalpable way, an air of vague satiation that conjugal life sometimes gives to men.

The power of this silent sedimentation into habit, which I had so feared during my relationship with him, seemed impregnable to me, justifying as it did the stub-bornness of those women who—at the risk of being annoyed, unsatisfied, or even unhappy—placed the man they wanted to keep into their furniture.

And when, on the telephone with him, I had the desire to revive the genre of murmured exchanges we used to have, "you like pussy, don't you—not any pussy, your pussy," etc, I resisted. For him these would just be tepid obscenities, unable to arouse him, since, like the married man approached by a whore, he would have been able to reply, "Thanks, but I have what I need at home."

More and more, at certain moments, it would occur to me fleetingly that I could put a stop to this possession, break the evil spell, as simply as one passes from one room into another or walks out into the street. But something more was needed, and I didn't know where it would come from—from chance, from the outside, or from within myself.

———

One afternoon, I was with him in a café near Saint-Phillipe-du-Roule. It was glacially cold and the café was poorly heated. From where I was sitting, I could see only my legs in one of the oval mirrors that bizarrely adorned the base of the counter. I had put on socks that were too short, and my pant leg, which had risen up, revealed a strip of white skin. It was every café in my life where I had been sad because of a man. This one was, as usual, evasive and prudent. We left each other at the Métro. He was going to pick up the other woman, to go home to an apartment which I would never know, to continue to live with her, in her intimacy, the way he had lived in mine. And walking down the stairs, I repeated to myself, this is too fucked up.

The next night I woke up with my heart beating violently. I had slept only an hour. There was something in me, a suffering, a madness, that I had to get rid of at all costs. I got up and walked over to the telephone. I dialed the number of his cell phone and said into the voice mail: "I don't want to see you anymore. But it's fine!" As happens with communication by satellite, I heard my voice echo in the distance, its artificially light tone accompanied by a little, crazy-sounding laugh. Returning to bed, I was still overwhelmed by suffering. It was too late to take a sleeping pill. I recalled and recited the prayers of my childhood, expecting I suppose that they would have the same effect they did then: grace, or calm. To the same end, I gave myself an orgasm. The expanse of pain before morning was infinite.

Lying on my stomach, I began to imagine words beneath me that had the consistency of stones, tablets of the law. But the letters were dancing and coming together, then breaking apart, like those that float in "alphabet" soup. I absolutely had to capture these words, they were the ones I needed to set myself free, there were no others. I was afraid they would escape me. As long as they were not written down, I would remain in my madness. I turned the light back on and scribbled them on the first page of the book on my bedside table: *Jane Eyre*. It was five o'clock. The question of sleep was immaterial. I had drafted my goodbye letter.

I cleaned it up in the morning—brief, concise, without any of the usual strategies and requesting no response. I thought to myself that I had just crossed the "Nuit du Walpurgis classique," even though I don't know the exact meaning of this title of a poem by Verlaine, the rest of which I have forgotten.

(To give a title to the moments of one's life, the way one does at school for literary passages, is perhaps a way to master them?)

He did not reply to the letter. After that, we telephoned each other from time to time, out of sheer habit. That too has ended.

When I do think of his cock, I see it the way it appeared to me the first night, crossing his stomach at the height of my eyes, in the bed where I lay on my side: big and powerful, bulging like a club at the tip. It's like an unknown cock in a scene I might see in a film.

I took an AIDS test. This had become a habit similar to the one I had as an adolescent, to go to confession—a sort of rite of purification.

I no longer have any desire to find out the name of the other woman or anything else about her (warning: I will decline up-front the solicitude of any potential informers).* I have stopped seeing her in the body of every woman I encounter. I am no longer on my guard when I'm walking in Paris. I no longer change the radio station when "Happy Wedding" comes on. I sometimes have the feeling I've lost something, a little like someone who realizes he no longer has the need to smoke or to take drugs.

Writing has been a way to save that which is no longer my reality—a sensation seizing me from head to foot,

* Who may have, for example, decoded the system of substitutions I have used—for the sake of discretion, or some basically conscientious reason—for the initials and any precise locations.

in the street—but has become "the possession," a period of time, circumscribed and completed.

I am through with trotting out the figures of jealousy, to which I was both prey and spectator; with inventorying the shared spaces that proliferated, impossible to control, in my mind; with describing all this spontaneous inner rhetoric, greedy and painful, determined to reach the truth whatever the cost; and through—because this is what it's really about—with happiness. I have succeeded in filling, with words, the absent image and name of the woman who for six months continued to put on her makeup, to go about her business, to talk and to enjoy herself, without suspecting that she was also living elsewhere, in the head and the skin of another woman.

———

I went back to Venice this summer. I revisited the campo San Stefan, the San Travaso church, the Montin restaurant, and of course the Zatters—all the places I had gone with W. There are no longer any flowers on the balcony of the room I had occupied with him in the Annex of the hotel La Calcina; the shutters were closed. Below, the iron grille of the café Cucciolo was lowered and the sign had disappeared. At La Calcina, they told me that the Annex had been closed for two years. It had probably been sold as apartments. I continued in the direction of the Douane de Mer, but it was inaccessible because of construction. I sat down along the wall of the Magasins du Sel, where the water overflows and stagnates in puddles on the embankment. Across the canal, on the Giudecca, the facades of San Giorgio and of Redentore were covered in canvas tarps. At the other end towered the black mass, intact, of the disused Mulino Stucky.

May–June & September–October 2001

ABOUT THE AUTHOR

Born in 1940, ANNIE ERNAUX grew up in Normandy. From 1977 to 2000, she was a professor at the Centre National d'Enseignement par Correspondance. In 1984, she won the Prix Renaudot for her book *La Place*. Eight of her novels have been published in America, including *A Woman's Story*, a *New York Times* Notable Book; and *A Man's Place*, a *New York Times* Notable Book and a finalist for the *Los Angeles Times* Book Prize. Some of her recent works include *L'événement* (2000), *Se perdre* (2001), and *L'usage de la photo* (2005). Ernaux's most recent book, *Les années*, is now a major bestseller in France, having sold in excess of 200,000 copies.